for Amy Thomas Crisafulli,
sister and mom extraordinaire,
whose idea it was.–ST

for Joe and baby Louisa.–TMW

Tricycle Press
a little division of Ten Speed Press
P.O. Box 7123, Berkeley, California 94707
www.tenspeed.com

Design by Jean Sanchirico
Typeset in Pike
The illustrations in this book were rendered in watercolor, gouache, colored pencils and collage.

Library of Congress Cataloging-in-Publication Data
Thomas, Scott.
The yawn heard 'round the world / by Scott Thomas ; illustrations by Tatjana Mai-Wyss.
p. cm.
Summary: A little girl who says she is not tired lets out a big yawn that spreads to others around the world before coming back to her house.
ISBN 1-58246-051-5
[1. Yawning--Fiction. 2. Stories in rhyme.] I. Mai-Wyss, Tatjana, 1972- ill. II. Title.
PZ8.3.T3166 Yaw 2003
[E]--dc21
2002007143

First Tricycle Press printing, 2003
Manufactured in China

2 3 4 5 6 — 07 06 05 04

The Yawn Heard 'Round the World

written by Scott Thomas
illustrations by Tatjana Mai-Wyss

Tricycle Press
Berkeley / Toronto

Her mother tucked her into bed,
but "I'm not sleepy," Sara said.
"I'm not through having fun today.
Let me stay up. I want to play!"

But then her mouth, it opened **wide** and something came from deep inside...

A yawn! A great big sleepy sound

and right away her mother found

that **she** was feeling sleepy, too.

So what could Sara's mother do?

She yawned.

And just across the hall

where Sara's dad had made a call,

he yawned as loudly as a tuba—
they heard it all the way in Cuba.

Aunt Lucy caught that yawny feeling,
and her yawn really shook the ceiling.

It scared a passing chickadee
so much he swooooped across the sea

to Paris, France. A solid hour
he yawned atop the Eiffel Tower.
Down below, the busy mayor
was honoring a soccer player.
Man looked up and bird looked down—
the mayor's yawn just rocked the town.

A lady with three fancy poodles
dug into her plate of noodles,

then plopped into a soggy snooze.
(They put it on the morning news.)

Whizzing by in a rattling taxi
a crazy driver, name of Maxie,
swerved to see that silly scene
and yawned so hard her eyes turned green.

In the back seat
an opera star
said sleepily,
"Speed up this car!
To the airport—drive like mad!"
And off he flew to sing in Chad.

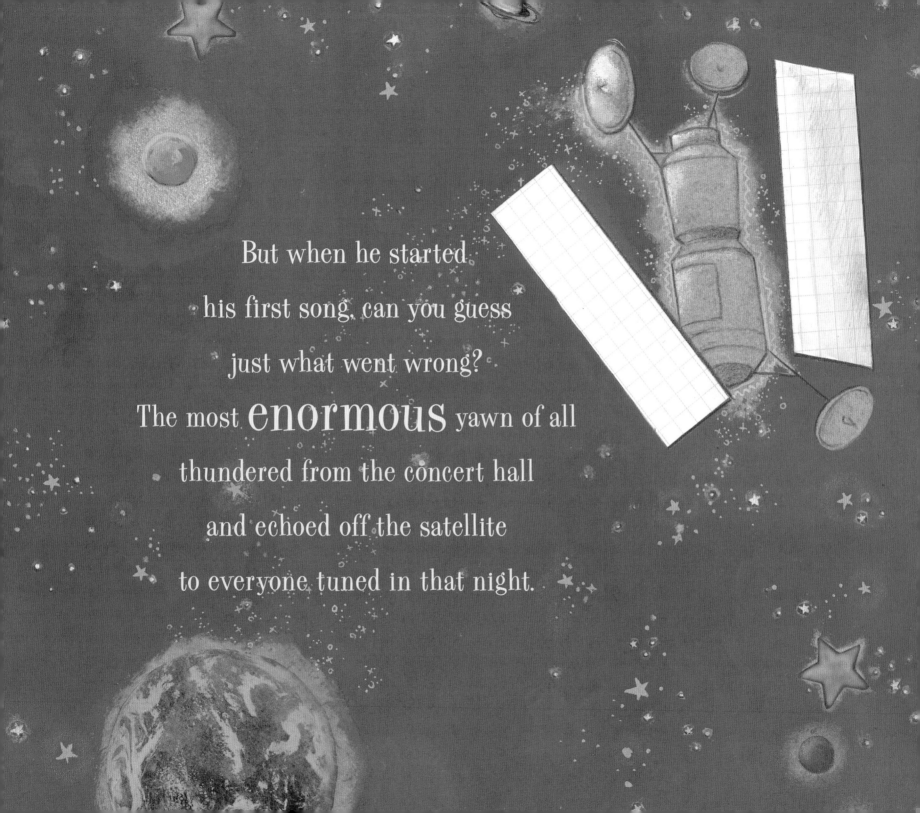

But when he started
his first song, can you guess
just what went wrong?
The most **enormous** yawn of all
thundered from the concert hall
and echoed off the satellite
to everyone tuned in that night.

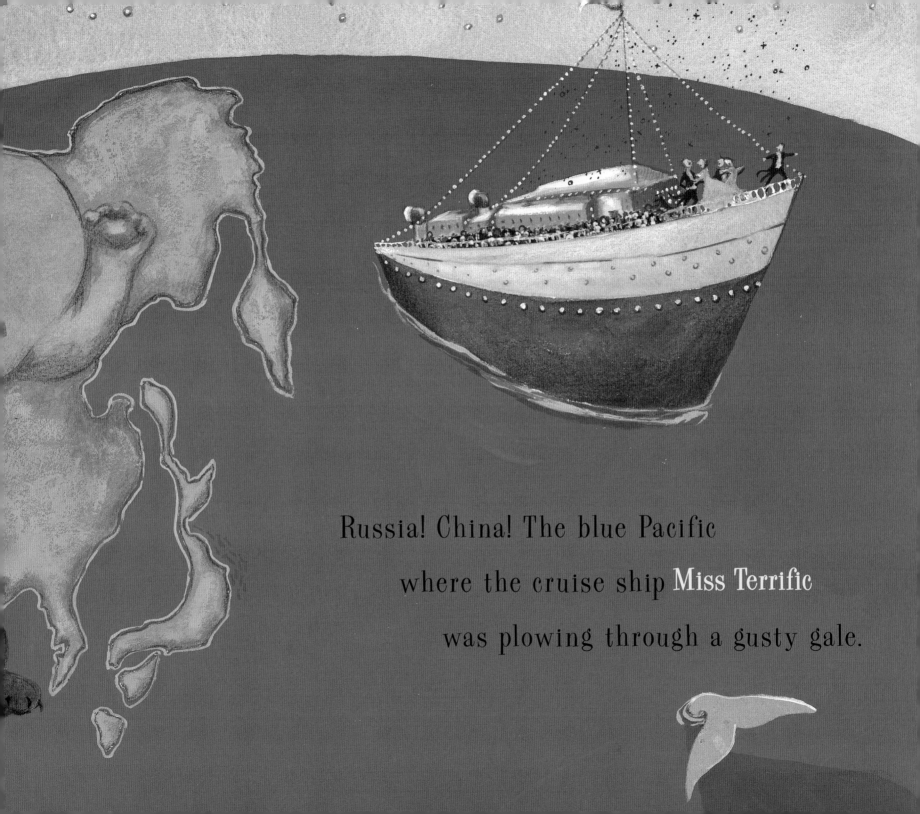

Russia! China! The blue Pacific

where the cruise ship Miss Terrific

was plowing through a gusty gale.

That yawn surprised a big blue whale
who did what whales quite often do
and swam swam swam
all the way to Peru.

The whale was oh so very tired,
and his humongous yawn inspired
a surfer on his daily ride
who yawned to shore on his backside.

Heading home, he stopped to watch
a swirl of horses, all top-notch.

It was the grand Paso parade! And as those beauties

pawed and neighed,

the surfer tried to button his lip
but-oops!-he let a small one slip.
A wave of yawning swept the crowd
which once had been so very loud.

Then all those yawns from far and wide

began a long and breezy ride

all the way to Sara's street

and to her house on windy feet. They mac